Samuel French Acting Edition

CW00537005

Squirrel Girl Goes to College

A Squirrel Girl Play

by Karen Zacarías

Based on the Marvel Comics *by* Will Murray & Steve Ditko

SAMUELFRENCH.COM SAMUELFRENCH.CO.UK

MUSIC USE NOTE

IMPORTANT BILLING AND CREDIT REQUIREMENTS

FOR MARVEL ENTERTAINMENT, INC.

Dan Buckley – President

Joe Quesada – Chief Creative Officer

Alan Fine – Executive Producer

Stephen Wacker – VP, Creative & Content Development

Sana Amanat – VP, Content & Character Development

Nick Lowe – Executive Editor, Vice President for Content, Digital Publishing

John Nee – Publisher

Mike Pasciullo – Senior Vice President, Global Marketing & Communications

Mitch Montgomery – Executive Director, Brand & Creative Operations

SPECIAL THANKS

CB Cebulski, David Bogart, Tim Cheng, Ashley Irving, Rickey Purdin, and Ellie Pyle, Darren Sanchez

ADDITIONAL CREDITS

Dramaturg

Ken Cerniglia

Contributors

Matt Hagmeier Curtis, Julie Haverkate, Pearl Hodiwala, Sarah Kenny, Janette Martinez, Lisa Mitchell, David Redman Scott, Democracy Prep Endurance High School (New York, NY), Holton-Arms School (Bethesda, MD), Marist School (Atlanta, GA), New World School of the Arts (Miami, FL), Northwest School of the Arts (Charlotte, NC), Riverton High School (Riverton, UT), Saint Ignatius High School (Cleveland, OH), Satellite High School Academy of Fine Arts (Satellite Beach, FL), Shadow Mountain High School (Phoenix, AZ), State College Area High School (State College, PA)

MARVEL SPOTLIGHT

Welcome, True Believers!

I'm so glad to have you join us and take your place amongst the legendary pantheon of Marvel heroes.

In the early 1960s, Marvel was a small, upstart comic book company introducing little-known characters like Spider-Man, The Avengers, Black Panther, and so many more that are household names today. It's been an exciting ride over the last 20 years as we've expanded from the printed page to animation, television, movies, and games. Complete and total world domination... well, almost. I've been fortunate enough to serve at Marvel during this time, first as Editor-in-Chief and now as Chief Creative Officer, and I firmly believe that our success in each of these mediums has come from our love for the characters and an unbridled excitement that we bring to each new challenge. That's why I can't begin to tell you how thrilled I am about Marvel Spotlight and your participation in it – it's going to be amazing to see you bring these stories to life.

Marvel Spotlight is an all-new way to experience some of the greatest heroes ever. But the best part is that we get to watch you interpret them in your own way as you expand the Marvel Universe into a whole new medium (yes, and *then* we can claim complete and utter world domination).

At Marvel we tell the stories of ordinary people doing extraordinary things and I can't wait to see what extraordinary things you'll bring to these stories. So now, if you'd indulge me, take a deep breath and say it with me, loud, so that they call down from hallowed halls of Asgard complaining about the noise: "Move over, Shakespeare! Take a seat, Chekhov! Here comes Marvel Spotlight!"

See ya in the funny books,

Joe Quesada
Chief Creative Officer
Marvel Entertainment, Inc.

THE ORIGIN OF SQUIRREL GIRL

Doreen Green bonded with squirrels at an early age and soon developed the ability to communicate with them. She just really loves squirrels, okay? Now as Squirrel Girl, she's got all the powers of a squirrel and all the powers of a girl! Sure, Doreen's enhanced, squirrel-like strength, speed, agility, and reflexes make her gifted at climbing, jumping, and other hand-to-hand combat. And, of course, with her squirrel partner and best friend, Tippy-Toe, she's fought alongside heroes like Iron Man and battled boisterous brutes like Doctor Doom. In her heart, though, she's just a young hero who's super excited about squirrels, nuts, and kickin' butts... oh, and justice.

AUTHOR'S NOTE

Comedy is a unique form of truth-telling. And also the hardest. Audiences usually cry about the same things; laughter and joy are hard-won. Comedy takes timing, tone, style, and commitment, but too few actors get a chance to practice their comedic skills. So I was thrilled to have the opportunity to write a full-fledged comedy about one of the greatest (yet relatively unknown) Marvel characters: Squirrel Girl!

Created by Will Murray and Steve Ditko, Squirrel Girl is my kind of super hero: smart, witty, generous, and confident. I love how Doreen Green embraces the gift of all of her human and squirrel abilities. Her can-do attitude is down-to-earth and inspiring. She cares about her friends, school, and environment and wants to make the world a better place. Squirrel Girl makes us realize that we all have super powers within – and that joy and laughter can be a powerful, unifying force for good.

And that theater that makes us laugh can also make us think.

Karen Zacarías

CHARACTERS

SQUIRREL CHORUS – They sing, they dance, they chant, they comment. May double as **STUDENTS, LITTLE TOMÁS, LITTLE NANCY, CHIPMUNK,** and **LITTLE GEORGIE**. Any gender.

TIPPY-TOE – Squirrel narrator. Doreen's best friend and crime-fighting partner. Female identifying

DOREEN GREEN – a.k.a. Squirrel Girl. Our hero, college freshman, positive, enthusiastic, protective. Female identifying.

DOCTOR DOOM – Obsessive, humorless super villain. Any gender.

TOMÁS LARA-PEREZ – College freshman, former cheerleader, Doreen's crush. Male identifying.

NANCY WHITEHEAD – College freshman, Doreen's dorm roommate. Female identifying.

BRIGHTMIND – Luminous computer science professor. Doubles as **GOOD TEACHER**. Any gender.

SMARTNOGGIN – Brightmind's offstage teaching assistant. Doubles as **MEAN TEACHER**. Any gender.

FREAK – Freaky new teaching assistant. Any gender.

MODOC – Suspicious substitute professor and super villain whose brain houses a giant computer. Any gender.

Marvel Spotlight aims to create compelling plays with teenage protagonists who tackle real-world problems in a diverse society. Licensees are encouraged to approach casting in a way that values equal representation and inclusion while promoting conversation and respect. Characters designated "any gender" should be costumed to reflect the gender identity of the performers.

SETTING

Empire State University

TIME

Present

PROLOGUE
Theater

(**TIPPY-TOE** *enters with* **SQUIRREL CHORUS.**)

CHORUS. *(sings a fierce theme song of their own creation)*
SQUIRREL GIRL, SUPER HERO
SHE'S THE STRONGEST ONE IN THE WORLD
SHE'S UP-FRONT! SHE'S POSITIVE!
FIGURING OUT THE BEST WAY TO LIVE
SQUIRREL GIRL, WATCH OUT!
HERE COMES SQUIRREL GIRL!

TIPPY-TOE. Today, dear friends, we present a dramatic work like no other.

SQUIRREL 1. This is a story of adventure, secrets, and truth.

CHORUS. Heck yeah!

SQUIRREL 2. It's a story of fierce female energy.

CHORUS. That's right!

SQUIRREL 3. And the power of squirrels!

CHORUS. Sensational *(sung)*
SQUIRRELS!

TIPPY-TOE. Starring:

(**DOREEN** *enters and takes place in line.*)

DOREEN. Doreen Green as our fabulous hero: Squirrel Girl.

CHORUS. Protagonist!

(**DOCTOR DOOM** *enters and takes place in line.*)

DOCTOR DOOM. *(reading script or program, confused)* Doctor Doom as... Baddie Number 2? Me? Doctor Doom? Really?

CHORUS. Antagonist... Number 2!

(**TOMÁS** *enters and takes place in line.*)

TOMÁS. Tomás Lara-Perez as Doreen's new college friend.

CHORUS. Potential Crush!

(**NANCY** *enters and takes place in line.*)

NANCY. Nancy Whitehead as Doreen's college roommate.

CHORUS. Potential Best Friend!

(**BRIGHTMIND** *enters and takes place in line.*)

BRIGHTMIND. Brightmind as the Engaged, Innovative, and Dynamic computer science professor.

CHORUS. Good Teacher!

(**MODOC** *enters and takes place in line.*)

MODOC. Modoc as the suspicious substitute computer science professor.

CHORUS. Antagonist... Number 1!

DOCTOR DOOM. Really??

TIPPY-TOE. And other characters to be introduced later or... presented in flashback.

CHORUS. Fabulous Flashback!

TIPPY-TOE. *(to audience)* I am Tippy-Toe, Squirrel Girl's long-time crime-fighting partner and best friend.

DOREEN. Tippy, only people with squirrel powers can understand you.

TIPPY-TOE. In our play, the audience can understand me because I have the coveted role of the narrator. And these sassy squirrels are the:

CHORUS. Greek chorus!

TIPPY-TOE. Now, let's get started.

(*All except* **TIPPY-TOE** *and* **CHORUS** *exit.*)

SCENE ONE
Empire State University

TIPPY-TOE. (*formally announces to the audience*) "Scene One: The Beginning."

SQUIRREL 1. Setting:

SQUIRREL 2. Empire State University.

SQUIRREL 3. Move-in day.

> (**DOREEN** *enters carrying a large box of clanking contents as if it were light as a feather.*)

DOREEN. I thought this day would never come.

SQUIRREL 2. What's in that big heavy box, Squirrel Girl?

DOREEN. Lots of nuts.

CHORUS. (*reveals slogan t-shirts*) Eat Nuts and Kick Butts!

TIPPY-TOE. Squirrel Girl Forever!

DOREEN. Except... don't call me Squirrel Girl here.

TIPPY-TOE. Oh, right... (*to audience*) "High School Graduation."

CHORUS. Flashback!

> (**DOREEN** *puts down her box to enter the flashback.* **TIPPY-TOE** *hands* **DOREEN** *a cap and gown with a huge squirrel tail as the* **CHORUS** *hums a sassy squirrel version of "Pomp and Circumstance."*)

DOREEN. I love this pompous song.

> (**DOCTOR DOOM** *enters.*)

DOCTOR DOOM. I am Doctor Doom!

CHORUS. Antagonist Number 2!

> (**DOCTOR DOOM** *sneers at the second-class designation.*)

DOCTOR DOOM. I am here to ensure my domination of the world by stopping you from graduating, Squirrel Girl!

DOREEN. A high school diploma is a powerful thing, and I've earned it.

DOCTOR DOOM. Stop graduating... or I will hurt your friends!

(**DOCTOR DOOM** *grabs* **TIPPY-TOE.**)

TIPPY-TOE. He's got me!

(**TIPPY-TOE** *bites* **DOCTOR DOOM.**)

DOCTOR DOOM. Ouch! You bit me!

(**DOREEN, TIPPY-TOE,** *and* **CHORUS** *strike a martial arts defensive pose against* **DOCTOR DOOM.** *Maybe they fight.*)

DOREEN. Doctor Doom, why are you intimidated by accomplished young women?

DOCTOR DOOM. Because you do good things!

DOREEN. You know... The Future Is Female—

DOCTOR DOOM. The Future Is... You Failing!

DOREEN. I overcame standardized testing, A.P. History, and Coach Grumby's health class to get here. You will not stop me from graduating!

(**DOREEN** *throws her cap in the air, maybe slo-mo.*)

DOCTOR DOOM. Nooooo!

CHORUS. *(sung)*

SHE GRADUATES! OH YEAH! SHE GRADUATES!

DOCTOR DOOM. I will find you in college, Squirrel Girl. And I will make you, and everyone you love, regret that you ever graduated high school! HA-HA-HA!

DOREEN. Not funny, Doctor Room.

DOCTOR DOOM. Doctor *Doom*!

DOREEN. You have bad comic timing, Doctor Zoom.

DOCTOR DOOM. Doom. Doom! DOOOOOOOOOOOM.

DOREEN. Because you have no patience, Doctor.

(**DOCTOR DOOM** *pauses, gets big, and then lets out a big laugh.*)

DOCTOR DOOM. "Patients, Doctor"... I get it! That's funny. But it also makes me—

(DOCTOR DOOM and CHORUS groan.)

DOREEN. It's what we call a "dad joke."

DOCTOR DOOM. I always wanted a dad.

DOREEN. Oh, I'm sorry. I didn't realize—

DOCTOR DOOM. Maybe my toxic personality results from the lack of positive role models.

DOREEN. *(super sensing something odd)* Doctor Doom... is that really you?

DOCTOR DOOM. If I had people who cared, people who made me laugh...

DOREEN. Why don't you take up comic improv? Maybe you need less "but no..." and more "Yes, *and...*"

DOCTOR DOOM. But no—

DOREEN. *(using trust as a tactic)* I've never said this to anyone, Doctor Doom, but I've always wanted a sibling.

DOCTOR DOOM. Well, you are an only child...

DOREEN. How did you know?

DOCTOR DOOM. *(whips out a Squirrel Girl comic book)* I studied you. At age twelve you began to discover you had the proportional strength and agility of a squirrel. You have an aptitude for numbers and a great can-do attitude. You are the only super hero in the world who has never been defeated, which is why you are my ultimate target!

DOREEN. Yeah, that's cool, but all I really want is to make great friends in college. Like really close friends.

DOCTOR DOOM. Squirrel Girl, how does one make close friends?

DOREEN. I'm not really sure.

DOCTOR DOOM. By sharing, perhaps?

DOREEN. But sharing... what?

DOCTOR DOOM. Let me share this advice: WATCH YOUR BACK. Because I will hunt you down in college and destroy your new "really close friends." HA-HA-HA!

> (**DOCTOR DOOM** *storms off.*)

CHORUS. End of flashback!

TIPPY-TOE. Hey! Why are you so hyped about new friends?

DOREEN. I love you, Tippy-Toe, but there are some human things that I think only another human would understand. Understand?

TIPPY-TOE. But no—

DOREEN. So now I'll just be Doreen Green so I can protect my new friends... that I don't have yet.

TIPPY-TOE. How are you going to make new friends if you can't be your squirrel self?

DOREEN. Doreen Green *is* myself!

TIPPY-TOE. Well, yeah, but not your whole self...

> (**DOREEN** *takes a deep breath and picks up her box.*)

SCENE TWO
Outside the Dorm

(TOMÁS enters.)

TOMÁS. Hello.

CHORUS. Tomás!

(TOMÁS startles DOREEN, and the box falls.)

TIPPY-TOE. Up next: "Doreen Meets Tomás."

CHORUS. Too cute!

TOMÁS. Hey. Are you okay?

DOREEN. I am okay. *(notices that TOMÁS is really cute)* I'm fine. I'm great. Wow. You're great. What? Awesome school, huh? Do your eyes always sparkle like that?

TOMÁS. Um... I came over to see if you needed help. I'm sorry I startled you.

DOREEN. No, I'm clumsy.

> *(DOREEN picks up the heavy box. We hear clanky noises within, maybe a "moo," or popping popcorn.)*

TOMÁS. *(flirty)* No, I am.

DOREEN. Okay... you are.

> *(DOREEN and TOMÁS do-si-do a little.)*

TOMÁS. *(laughs)* I like this little dance.

DOREEN. But no. I don't dance. *(laughs and lets the box fall again)* You know, my poor popcorn popper isn't going to survive this day.

TOMÁS. I'm so sorry.

DOREEN. Oh... it's okay. Who needs popcorn?

TOMÁS. It's a carb. And a grain. And delicious.

CHORUS. Mmm... popcorn...

DOREEN. Did you know a single kernel pops with such force it can be propelled up to three feet in the air?

TOMÁS. Cool. I'm Tomás. And you are?

CHORUS. (*jazz hands*) Squirrel Girl!

> (**DOREEN** *gestures "Quiet!"* **CHORUS** *freezes – oops.*)

DOREEN. My name is Doreen. Doreen Green. I'm moving in.

TOMÁS. I moved in yesterday.

DOREEN. Are you a first-year too?

TOMÁS. Yep, freshman – majoring in computer science!

DOREEN. Me too! I so want to study with Professor Brightmind.

TOMÁS. Me too! Brightmind is considered the best teacher in the field.

DOREEN. Engaged!

TOMÁS. Innovative!

TOMÁS & DOREEN. And Dynamic!

DOREEN. I've always wanted to bridge the worlds of technology and human psychology.

TOMÁS. Yes! Artificial intelligence can improve the world when coupled with human compassion.

DOREEN. Coupled. For sure.

TOMÁS. Amazing. I wonder what more we have in common.

DOREEN. Well... I like squirrels.

TOMÁS. I like chipmunks.

DOREEN. Ha-ha-ha.

TOMÁS. Ha-*ha*-ha. Here, let me help with this box.

> (**TOMÁS** *tries to pick up the box but can't.* **DOREEN** *quickly and easily takes it in her arm.*)

DOREEN. No! I got it. No worries. See you in class tomorrow.

TOMÁS. You are strong, girl!

DOREEN. I mean, yeah, I am strong, but like in a kick-ass, girls-belong-in-the-House-and-the-Senate-and-the-White-House kind of way... not in like a woo-hoo-super-hero way. Like, I'm totally outstanding, but still a regular human.

TOMÁS. Totally, a regular human.

DOREEN. And I've never had a boyfriend. Like, I've kissed a guy, but never like been really committed to a relationship – argghhh!

CHORUS. Awkward!

DOREEN. Um. Yeah. Okay. Bye.

TOMÁS. Bye.

*(**DOREEN** goes to her dorm.)*

SCENE THREE
Dorm

TIPPY-TOE. "Doreen Meets Nancy."

CHORUS. In the dorm!

NANCY. So *you're* my new roommate?

CHORUS. She's got attitude!

TIPPY-TOE. That's good, right?

DOREEN. Yes! My name is—

CHORUS. *(jazz hands) Not* Squirrel Girl!

DOREEN. I am Doreen Green.

NANCY. So you met Tomás, huh? I saw you through the window.

DOREEN. Who? Oh, you mean the totally hot, cute personable guy who spoke to me in a warm, inquisitive, and respectful manner?

NANCY. Yeah, him.

DOREEN. Didn't notice.

        (**NANCY** *and* **DOREEN** *laugh.*)

TIPPY-TOE. *(jealous?)* Wow, they're sure bonding fast...

NANCY. Here, let me help you. *(overwhelmed)* What's in here? So heavy!

DOREEN. Nuts!

CHORUS. Nuts Kick Butts!

NANCY. That's a lot of nuts.

TIPPY-TOE. So judgmental!

DOREEN. Macadamia, pistachio, almonds, walnuts...

NANCY. Are you some kind of squirrel or something?

CHORUS. Or something!

DOREEN. I'm just really into all the omegas. Walnuts really deliver.

NANCY. Well, good thing I'm not allergic.

TIPPY-TOE. About one in eight people in the U.S. are allergic to nuts.

CHORUS. More nuts for us!

DOREEN. Plus I have my pet squirrel, Tippy-Toe.

TIPPY-TOE. That's me!

NANCY. Oh no. I am not a fan of rodents.

CHORUS. What??

TIPPY-TOE. How dare she!

NANCY. I think I am allergic. Excuse me, while I—

> (**NANCY** *sneezes in a very dramatic fashion,
> maybe slo-mo.*)

CHORUS. Achoo-hoo!

DOREEN. Tippy, I'm sorry.

TIPPY-TOE. What?

DOREEN. I think you can't live here in the dorm.

CHORUS. *Et tu, Brute?*

TIPPY-TOE. I am your best friend!

DOREEN. I am sorry Tippy... but you are going to have to live outside.

TIPPY-TOE. In a tree???

CHORUS. Gasp!

DOREEN. You've always lived in a tree! You are a squirrel. Not a girl.

TIPPY-TOE. And you are Squirrel Girl!

CHORUS. Shhh!

> (**DOREEN** *opens a "window."* **TIPPY-TOE** *climbs
> outside and presses her nose against the
> "glass."*)

DOREEN. *(to* **NANCY***)* I came to school to make lifelong friends.

NANCY. And I came here to study with Professor Brightmind.

DOREEN. Me too! Professor Brightmind is considered the best teacher in the field.

NANCY. Engaged!

DOREEN. Innovative!

NANCY & DOREEN. And Dynamic!

NANCY. I wonder what else we have in common?

TIPPY-TOE. *(evil eye)* I see you!

SCENE FOUR
Classroom

TIPPY-TOE. (*through "window"*) "Professor Brightmind's Amazing Computer Science 101 Class. Day One."

> (**DOREEN, TOMÁS,** *and* **NANCY** *appear in the classroom.* **CHORUS** *fills in as other* **STUDENTS.**)

DOREEN. Tomás... Nancy. Nancy... Tomás.

NANCY. Our first college class ever!

TOMÁS. Empire U!

DOREEN. It's going to be epic!

> (**BRIGHTMIND** *enters.*)

BRIGHTMIND. Hello, students. I am Professor Brightmind.

> (**CHORUS** *lips fanfare.*)

I love my first years... because your young, bright minds are our future. I strive to be Engaged, Innovative...

TOMÁS, DOREEN & NANCY. And Dynamic!

BRIGHTMIND. Please meet my fabulous teaching assistant, Smartnoggin...

CHORUS. Offstage!

SMARTNOGGIN. (*offstage*) Hello.

BRIGHTMIND. Smartnoggin is down the hall, wiring the classroom computers to better assist us.

SMARTNOGGIN. (*offstage*) Yes, I am!

BRIGHTMIND. Now... we journey into the programmatic puzzle that is computer science. So grab on to your logic... and open your imagination. Are you ready to learn?

STUDENTS. Yeah!

BRIGHTMIND. I didn't hear you. Are you ready to learn?

STUDENTS. Yeah!

BRIGHTMIND. One more time. Are you ready to learn?

(Full pep rally energy. **CHORUS** *might even pull out pom-poms.)*

STUDENTS. Yeah!

BRIGHTMIND. *(chants)* Computer...

STUDENTS. Science!

BRIGHTMIND. Computer...

STUDENTS. Science!

BRIGHTMIND. Computer...

STUDENTS. Science!

BRIGHTMIND. Wonderful. Let's begin...

SCENE FIVE
Dorm

CHORUS. "Bonding in the Dorm."

TIPPY-TOE. *(still outside the "window")* Don't mind me here, outside!

CHORUS. Like a squirrel!

DOREEN. Wow, that class was... *(to* **TOMÁS***)* Engaging...

NANCY. Innovative!

TOMÁS & DOREEN. And Dynamic!

TIPPY-TOE. It's so windy out here!

TOMÁS. I've never had a teacher like that.

NANCY. I had a soccer coach like that. He was so enthusiastic. He was also my dad. But I am not sporty at all and turned out to be the worst player on the team.

DOREEN. Oh no!

NANCY. I mean, I'm glad I *tried* soccer, because it made me realize what I really wanted to play...

CHORUS. What?

NANCY. I promised myself I wouldn't tell anyone at college.

TOMÁS. You can tell us.

NANCY. The harmonica.

DOREEN. Harmonica? Cool!

TIPPY-TOE. Not cool.

CHORUS. *(sung)*
    HARMONICA *IS* COOL!

NANCY. I just love it. But don't tell anyone.

DOREEN. Okay. Do you have a secret, Tomás?

TOMÁS. *(reluctantly, deep breath)* Okay. My parents put me in little kid football, but I hated it – all that equipment and pounding and aggression. It was during a game that I looked over and... found my true calling.

CHORUS. What was it?

TOMÁS. Nobody here knows.

NANCY. Okay...

TOMÁS. *(whispers)* Cheerleading.

CHORUS. *(whispers)* Go team!

TOMÁS. I looked at the cheerleaders flying through the air and thought: Now, that looks fun. So I became a cheerleader. I love flipping out! And I got so good they asked me to try out for the Olympics.

TIPPY-TOE. Olympics... whatever.

NANCY. Did you go?

TOMÁS. *(looks away)* Nah...

NANCY. What about you, Doreen?

DOREEN. What about me?

TIPPY-TOE. Are you going to tell them you've always wanted a sibling? Or tell them you dance alone in your room because you have no rhythm? Or tell them you are a super hero?

CHORUS. Are you??

TIPPY-TOE. Or are you going to "protect" them?

DOREEN. Listen, I'm just really... ordinary.

TOMÁS. What does that mean?

NANCY. There must be something that makes you unique.

DOREEN. Nah, nothing to tell.

NANCY. You mean nothing to *share*... which is different.

TOMÁS. Doreen Green... girl of mystery.

DOREEN. A boring mystery.

TIPPY-TOE. *(to* **CHORUS,** *shifting tactics)* Tomás and Nancy seem... displeased. So maybe Doreen is right. Maybe the less she shares with these... humans, the better!

CHORUS. Really?

TIPPY-TOE. Really!

CHORUS. Okay...

SCENE SIX
Classroom

CHORUS. "Let's Program a Tree."

BRIGHTMIND. So if artificial intelligence can help us clone a tree, how would you program the bark?

TOMÁS. I would use x to code in concentric circles!

BRIGHTMIND. Wonderful! And Nancy... how would you formulate the sap?

NANCY. I got 2p times y for the sap.

BRIGHTMIND. Excellent. And if you take what you learned from those two equations... what happens then?

DOREEN. Oh! I know! I know!

BRIGHTMIND. Doreen?

DOREEN. The x becomes a sustainable line of code for the roots.

BRIGHTMIND. Amazing! So theoretically we can clone an entire tree?

DOREEN. Yes... but I don't think it would have any seeds. It would not be able to replicate itself...

BRIGHTMIND. Because life requires diversity. All clones are exactly the same.

DOREEN. Are they?

TOMÁS. Um... *clones*...

NANCY. So artificial intelligence might be able to create a tree—

DOREEN. But not a nut!

CHORUS. Gasp!

TIPPY-TOE. *(outside the "window")* Then what's the point?

SCENE SEVEN
Dorm

CHORUS. "The Friendship Blooms."

TIPPY-TOE. *(to* **CHORUS***)* You are killing me here.

TOMÁS. I've never learned so much in one day.

NANCY & DOREEN. Me neither.

NANCY. If only I could show my mean first grade teacher!

DOREEN. You had a mean first grade teacher?

TOMÁS. Me too!

NANCY. You can't tell anyone this story...

TOMÁS & DOREEN. Promise!

NANCY. So my mean first grade teacher said this to me:

CHORUS. Flashback!

> *(Enter* **MEAN TEACHER***. A* **SQUIRREL** *steps forward as* **LITTLE NANCY***. Or* **NANCY** *becomes little in some way.)*

MEAN TEACHER. Nancy? Read the next sentence.

LITTLE NANCY. Ummm... "The wane is in pains—"

MEAN TEACHER. Wrong! You are a terrible student, little Nancy. You will never amount to anything. I am failing you.

> *(***MEAN TEACHER** *exits.)*

LITTLE NANCY. Oh no! I'm a first grade failure!

DOREEN. That's rough. So, what happened?

NANCY. I had to repeat first grade.

TOMÁS. Oh no!

LITTLE NANCY. I'll never be a good student.

NANCY. But then I met a *good* teacher.

> *(Enter* **GOOD TEACHER***.)*

GOOD TEACHER. Nancy, please try again.

LITTLE NANCY. "The insane is in pains."

GOOD TEACHER. You are squinting... perhaps you need glasses.

(A SQUIRREL gently places glasses on LITTLE NANCY's face.)

LITTLE NANCY. Thank you, Good Teacher. I can see better. "The plain is pains."

GOOD TEACHER. And... I think you're inverting some of the letters. It's called dyslexia. We just have to teach your brain how to decipher what your eyes see so your mind can read correctly.

(GOOD TEACHER gently moves LITTLE NANCY's finger over the words.)

LITTLE NANCY. "The plain is in Spain!"

GOOD TEACHER. You got it!

CHORUS. End of flashback!

TOMÁS. That's why you're so good at code...

NANCY. Yeah, by learning how to unscramble words in my brain, I learned to unscramble other problems too.

TOMÁS. That's like a super hero skill!

DOREEN. You know... it really could be.

NANCY. I guess...

TOMÁS. Well, I'm going to tell you something, but you can't share it with anybody.

NANCY & DOREEN. Promise!

TOMÁS. There's a reason I didn't go to the Olympics.

NANCY. What was it?

TOMÁS. When I was a kid...

CHORUS. Another flashback!

(A SQUIRREL steps forward as LITTLE TOMÁS and skips by GOOD TEACHER.)

GOOD TEACHER. Hey, little kid... don't go over to the pond. It's full of green goop that leaked from that pharmaceutical factory. Bye.

(GOOD TEACHER exits.)

LITTLE TOMÁS. Thank you, Good Teacher. Wait... there's a chipmunk drinking from the pond!

CHORUS. Chipmunk!

> *(Another* **SQUIRREL** *steps forward as* **CHIPMUNK.***)*

LITTLE TOMÁS. Hey, cute little chipmunk... don't drink that green water. It's bad for you.

> *(***CHIPMUNK** *makes chipmunk noises and keeps drinking.* **LITTLE TOMÁS** *tries to pull* **CHIPMUNK** *away from the pond. The* **CHIPMUNK** *bites him.)*

Ouch. Why did you bite me? I was only trying to help you.

CHIPMUNK. I'm sorry. You startled me.

LITTLE TOMÁS. Hey. Why can I suddenly understand you?

CHIPMUNK. I don't know.

LITTLE TOMÁS. And why do I suddenly want to do this?

> *(***LITTLE TOMÁS** *performs a feat of great agility.)*

CHIPMUNK. Beats me.

LITTLE TOMÁS. And why do I suddenly feel very, very sick?

> *(***LITTLE TOMÁS** *performs a feat of great sickness.)*

DOREEN. Was it rabies?

CHORUS. Rabies!

TOMÁS. I got all these shots. Like in my stomach and everywhere.

NANCY & DOREEN. Ouch!

TOMÁS. But it wasn't rabies. I got better... but I changed.

NANCY. How?

> *(***LITTLE TOMÁS** *performs a feat of great gymnastics.)*

LITTLE TOMÁS. I can do gymnastics! Like crazy good. Like Olympic good.

> *(***MEAN TEACHER** *enters.)*

MEAN TEACHER. Little Tomás, we have the results of your blood test.

LITTLE TOMÁS. Okay!

MEAN TEACHER. Have you been taking something to enhance your performance?

LITTLE TOMÁS. No. But I got rabies shots after a chipmunk bite—

MEAN TEACHER. You *fail*! You are banned from the Olympics, banned from gymnastics, and banned from cheering ever again!

NANCY. Whoa. I'm sorry.

TOMÁS. So I never cheered again.

CHORUS. Boo team!

DOREEN. So Mean Teacher punished you because you're a chipmunk... hunk?

CHORUS. Chipmunk Hunk!

DOREEN. Wait... did I just say that out loud?

TIPPY-TOE. Oh yes you did.

TOMÁS. *(smiles)* I've never told anyone that story before. It's totally embarrassing. Please keep it confidential.

DOREEN. Of course!

NANCY. That's what friends are for. You can trust us.

(**TOMÁS** *and* **NANCY** *look at* **DOREEN**.)

DOREEN. Wow. I've never had a heart-to-heart like this with other humans before.

NANCY. Because you usually hang with squirrels?

TIPPY-TOE & CHORUS. Not anymore!

DOREEN. And super villains... but you know... ha-ha...

TOMÁS. You are so funny!

NANCY. You are always making jokes, Doreen. But, you really can talk to us.

TOMÁS. Yes! We are friends no matter what. There's nothing you can't tell us.

DOREEN. Really? Well... I want to share this secret—

TIPPY-TOE. (*jealousy taking over*) Doreen! Stop! Don't reveal yourself to these "humans."

DOREEN. But we are sharing...

TIPPY-TOE. What about Doctor Doom? You want to expose your "friends" to danger? And risk them rejecting you?

DOREEN. Reject me?

TIPPY-TOE. Yes, *and*—

DOREEN. But no!

CHORUS. Dramatic tension!

DOREEN. (*to* **TOMÁS** *and* **NANCY**) Sorry, friends. I got nothing.

TOMÁS. Nothing?

NANCY. Nothing?

CHORUS. Nothing!

DOREEN. Oh, I know. I have buck teeth. See? Oh, please don't tell anyone. Oh... wait! Everyone can see them, gosh darn it!

TOMÁS. (*laughs*) You are so funny! And so cute.

NANCY. (*skeptical*) You sure are...

(**TIPPY-TOE** *gets a win. For now.*)

SCENE EIGHT
Classroom

CHORUS. "What the Nuts?!"

BRIGHTMIND. So today's lesson... if a tree cloned by a computer falls in the forest and no one sees it... was it ever a tree?

(A knock on the door.)

What a freakish knock...

(FREAK enters.)

Please don't interrupt our Engaging, Innovative, and Dynamic classroom.

FREAK. I'm Freak, the new teacher's assistant.

BRIGHTMIND. My T.A. is Smartnoggin, whom I selected out of a very competitive applicant pool.

FREAK. I play video games...

SMARTNOGGIN. *(offstage)* Professor Brightmind! I need your help!

BRIGHTMIND. Of course. Always happy to help. One moment, class.

(BRIGHTMIND exits. Sounds of a professor-napping offstage.)

Help!

CHORUS. Uh-oh.

(MODOC enters.)

MODOC. Hello, class.

DOREEN. What happened to Professor Brightmind?

MODOC. Brightmind is... on sabbatical.

TOMÁS. Huh?

NANCY. Huh?

CHORUS. Huh?

MODOC. I am your substitute, Professor Modoc. M-O-D-O-C: Mobile Organism Designed Only for Computing.

CHORUS. Uh-oh.

MODOC. I hear that you are the smartest students at Empire State University. So I know you will figure out this problem... *(unveils a ridiculous cartoon-exclamation equation)* by tomorrow!

DOREEN, NANCY & TOMÁS. Tomorrow??

DOREEN. But that problem is a hard nut to crack!

MODOC. Exactly. Class dismissed.

FREAK. Get out of here, you pesky kids!

> *(*CHORUS *scatters.* TOMÁS, NANCY, *and*
> DOREEN *exit.)*

TIPPY-TOE. "The Evil Villain Monologue: smart, delusional, and zero self-doubt."

FREAK. Perfect. Let me tell you all about how I, Freak, came to be—

MODOC. Not you, Freak. The Evil Villain Monologue is all mine!

FREAK. Villains are so selfish!

MODOC. Little does anyone know I've secretly employed the talents of Smartnoggin...

SMARTNOGGIN. *(offstage)* Offstage!

MODOC. ...to monitor Brightmind's students. Nancy has the uncanny ability to scramble and unscramble code. Tomás masters gymnastics of the body and mind. And Doreen... well, she's just an ordinary kid with buck teeth and trust issues, but she can lure the others. Those smart, ambitious kids will spend all night trying to solve the problem. Their brain electricity and close friendship will create a priceless algorithm. Tomorrow I will connect their brains to mine, suck out all their knowledge, and turn it into code to conquer the world! *(emits artificial computer laugh)* HA-HA-HA!

FREAK. Freaky!

TIPPY-TOE. Delusional!

MODOC. Thank you!

> *(*MODOC *bows.)*

TIPPY-TOE. Moving on...

SCENE NINE
Dorm

CHORUS. "The Moment of Truth."

(Back in the dorm...)

TOMÁS. Cool that Professor Brightmind got a surprise sabbatical!

DOREEN. Something seems fishy to me. Why would Brightmind take off without telling us?

NANCY. Listen, subs happen.

TOMÁS. And this sub believes that we can solve this incredible problem. What a challenge!

DOREEN. I think Modoc is up to no good.

NANCY. Why are you so suspicious, Doreen?

TOMÁS. Do you know something we don't know?

TIPPY-TOE. Are your squirrel senses tingling?

DOREEN. *(makes funny tingling moves)* Maybe I'm just imagining things.

NANCY. Hey, Tomás, I just had an idea. Let's check out Professor Modoc's strange midnight office hours.

TOMÁS. This could be our chance to make real computer-science history!

DOREEN. Go ahead. I'll catch up. Just need a minute.

NANCY. Doreen, what are you holding back?

DOREEN. I am just an ordinary...

TOMÁS. *(heartbroken)* Let's go, Nancy.

(TOMÁS and NANCY exit.)

DOREEN. ... girl who dances badly, wants friends, and is a super hero...

TIPPY-TOE. "The Hero Dialogue: full of reflection, misgivings, and lots of self-doubt."

CHORUS. *(cheers)* Go self-doubt!

(TIPPY-TOE stares at CHORUS, who shrugs.)

DOREEN. To be or not to be? I've never felt as connected to people as I do to Tomás and Nancy. It's been so great to grow up with squirrelly friends... but now that I'm an adult, real human friends are...

TIPPY-TOE & CHORUS. Are what???

DOREEN. They're just... human. They have great gifts and abilities... and vulnerabilities. I would love to tell them about Squirrel Girl, but what if they freak out?

TIPPY-TOE. They might.

DOREEN. What if the truth creates distance?

TIPPY-TOE. Could happen.

DOREEN. What if my secret is just... a burden to them?

TIPPY-TOE. Could be a heavy one.

DOREEN. Oh, Tippy. You're right.

TIPPY-TOE. *(smugly satisfied)* Yes, I am. I'm the only one who can understand you. All of you.

DOREEN. Maybe it's too dangerous for me to have human friends.

CHORUS. Whoa!

TIPPY-TOE. Wait. What?

DOREEN. I just want to do what's right!

CHORUS. Do the right thing!

TIPPY-TOE. Doreen...

DOREEN. Help me pack, Tippy. Please.

TIPPY-TOE. You are going to leave the dorm?

DOREEN. I can live in a tree. With you.

TIPPY-TOE. But what about your education?

DOREEN. I can take online classes. By myself. In a tree.

TIPPY-TOE. What about your new friends?

DOREEN. They are better off without me.

CHORUS. Tippy! What have you done?

TIPPY-TOE. *(takes this all in, then:)* Doreen, I'm sorry! I've been jealous of your new friends because I've always considered you and me best friends.

DOREEN. But you and I will always be friends, Tippy-Toe.

TIPPY-TOE. I think you need to trust your instincts... and trust your new friends.

DOREEN. But there are risks!

TIPPY-TOE. Yes, *and* there are rewards!

(**DOREEN** *runs off.*)

What if I have messed up Doreen's life forever?

CHORUS. That would be bad.

SCENE TEN
Classroom

TIPPY-TOE. "The Confrontation!"

MODOC. My plan for world domination is almost realized. All I need is...

> (**TOMÁS** *and* **NANCY** *enter.*)

NANCY. Professor Modoc?

TOMÁS. We have ideas to run by you!

MODOC. Ah, just in time for me to absorb your unique talents and take over the world!

TOMÁS & NANCY. What?!?

TOMÁS. Doreen was right!

NANCY. There *was* something suspicious going on!

MODOC. Now, freeze!

> (*Zap!* **TOMÁS** *and* **NANCY** *freeze in place.*)

TOMÁS & NANCY. We are frozen in place!

MODOC. Smartnoggin just sent an electric stun pulse to your muscles.

TOMÁS & NANCY. Smartnoggin?!

SMARTNOGGIN. Offstage!

MODOC. Now, Freak, do your thing.

FREAK. This is all getting so freaky!

> (**FREAK** *places wired helmets on* **TOMÁS** *and* **NANCY.***)

MODOC. Your extraordinary talents will now be mine!

DOREEN. *(offstage)* Not so fast!

NANCY. Doreen!

TOMÁS. Doreen!

CHORUS. Doreen Green!

> (*Enter* **DOREEN** *as* **SQUIRREL GIRL** *tingling with squirrel energy.*)

DOREEN. Yes, *and* Squirrel Girl!

ALL. What?!?

TIPPY-TOE. Oh, thank nuts!

DOREEN. I know you all thought I was just a computer-science-loving girl. I am also a super hero.

MODOC. Huh. A bonanza!

TOMÁS. Why didn't you tell us?

DOREEN. I wanted to protect you.

NANCY. Protect us? How?

TOMÁS. We told you our deepest secrets, and you were always like, "Nothing."

NANCY. But you're a super hero?

TOMÁS. That's not cool, Doreen.

MODOC. Squirrel Girl, stand still so I can freeze you!

DOREEN. You don't understand...

NANCY. Don't you trust us?

TOMÁS. You think it was easy to open up?

DOREEN. You were so brave, telling me your stories.

FREAK. What stories?

CHORUS. Shh!

TOMÁS. Glad you enjoyed them.

NANCY. I think I could actually live with a rodent...

TIPPY-TOE. You could?

CHORUS. Progress!

NANCY. But I can't be roommates with someone who doesn't trust me. I think you were protecting *yourself.*

DOREEN. I thought revealing Squirrel Girl would bring trouble for people I cared about, but trouble seems to have found us anyway. I'm sorry. I want you to trust me.

TOMÁS. Then you have to trust us to handle your secrets, too.

NANCY. We're stronger than you think.

DOREEN. Okay. Here goes: I'm a super hero who dances weird because I have no rhythm.

NANCY & TOMÁS. Okay...

DOREEN. And I've always wanted a friend who felt like a sister.

NANCY. I can do that.

CHORUS. Sisters!

DOREEN. And I thought I also wanted a brother, except...

TOMÁS. Except, what?

DOREEN. I really don't want you to be like a brother.

CHORUS. Oooh...

TOMÁS. So you just want me to be like a... friend?

DOREEN. Yes, *and...*

TOMÁS. And??

TIPPY-TOE. The suspense is killing me.

MODOC. Enough! Freak, grab that squirrel... child.

FREAK. Now? I thought we were all sharing...

DOREEN. Did your parents name you Freak?

FREAK. Well... I was born a small child—

MODOC. Wait! I'm the super villain here. I get the monologue. Again!

TIPPY-TOE. "The Evil Villain Monologue, Part Two: The Scary Sob Story."

MODOC. I was born a small child by the name of Georgie Tarelton...

CHORUS. Flashback!

> (*A* **SQUIRREL** *steps forward to play* **LITTLE GEORGIE**.)

LITTLE GEORGIE. I am Little Georgie and I am cute.

> (**MEAN TEACHER** *enters.*)

MEAN TEACHER. I am your first grade teacher. And you are a failure.

LITTLE GEORGIE. But I'm just a kid.

MEAN TEACHER. If you fail, I fail. So don't fail. Maybe if I give you this goopy green pond water and connect you to this computer... you will be able to get to the second grade.

NANCY. That mean first grade teacher sounds familiar.

> (**MEAN TEACHER** *hands* **LITTLE GEORGIE** *a sippy cup and connects the child to a box.*)

LITTLE GEORGIE. Yummy.

MEAN TEACHER. Testing starts... now.

> (*The box ends up on* **LITTLE GEORGIE**'*s head.*)

LITTLE GEORGIE. Wait... my head is now a computer!

TIPPY-TOE. End of flashback!

MODOC. And by a series of computer experiments gone wrong... I became who and what I am now: MODOC. But now I will change my name to MODOC!

NANCY. That's the same name.

MODOC. But the "C" for Computing will become... Conquering!

TOMÁS. These names are not healthy.

MODOC. I will prove to you computers can do everything better than humans... humans you will soon cease to be!

NANCY. That's dark.

TOMÁS. Very dark.

FREAK. I'm freaked out!

DOREEN. You want to bet?

MODOC. Sure! How about a... dance-off?

DOREEN. Not a dance-off!

MODOC. I win.

NANCY & TOMÁS. Modoc can't win!

DOREEN. But dance? In public? That's my greatest fear!

NANCY. What if I play the harmonica?

CHORUS. Oooh!

TOMÁS. And I cheer you on?

CHORUS. Go Tomás!

FREAK. I love Broadway musicals!

CHORUS. (*sung*)
> START SPREADING THE NEWS...

TOMÁS. You aren't alone, Doreen.

NANCY. We have your back.

DOREEN. You're my heroes.

MODOC. Fine. Unfreeze the kids!

> (*NANCY and* **TOMÁS** *unfreeze and remove their wired helmets.* **TIPPY-TOE** *and* **FREAK** *move into judge positions.*)

TIPPY-TOE. Now, pop the popcorn.

CHORUS. We poppin'!

> (**CHORUS** *creates a great poppin' beat.* **NANCY** *plays harmonica.* **TOMÁS** *cheers.* **DOREEN** *dances awkwardly awesome.*)

TOMÁS. No way can Modoc beat that beat.

TIPPY-TOE. That was amazing!

FREAK. I give it a thumbs up.

MODOC. Give me a robot beat.

> (**CHORUS** *makes computer beep sounds in rhythm.* **MODOC** *does a surprisingly impressive robot dance.*)

ALL. Wow...

FREAK. I didn't think Modoc would pull it off.

TIPPY-TOE. What lacked in soul was made up in style!

TOMÁS. Humans, One. Computers, One.

NANCY. Tied.

MODOC. I win. Now I will drain you!

> (**BRIGHTMIND** *enters.*)

BRIGHTMIND. That's not how a tie works.

ALL. Professor Brightmind!

CHORUS. Good Teacher!

BRIGHTMIND. Someone blindfolded and tied me up offstage. Who would do such a thing?

> (**SMARTNOGGIN** *enters.*)

SMARTNOGGIN. Me!

BRIGHTMIND. Smartnoggin?

NANCY. Wait!

TOMÁS. You?

MODOC. You!

CHORUS. Mean Teacher!

SMARTNOGGIN. Ha! You are all failures!! I've been tormenting you for years... undermining your confidence and dreams to keep your passions and talents hidden – so now I can drain them and increase my power!!!

MODOC. You meany!

FREAK. I'm so freaked out.

DOREEN. Not so fast, Mean Teacher. My squirrel senses are tingling!

> (**DOCTOR DOOM** *enters holding an unplugged extension cord.*)

Perfect timing, Doctor Doom.

CHORUS. Doctor Doom!

DOCTOR DOOM. *(to* **SMARTNOGGIN***)* Is this what was holding your whole evil-wired plan together?

SMARTNOGGIN. Ugh. Nobody can beat Doctor Doom!

DOCTOR DOOM. Nobody, except Squirrel Girl.

DOREEN. Doctor... you look less doomy!

DOCTOR DOOM. I've been taking improv classes.

ALL. Really?

DOCTOR DOOM. Yes, *and* they have really helped me.

FREAK. I don't get it.

DOCTOR DOOM. I have found my true self. In this moment. Onstage. In this play.

CHORUS. A Squirrel Girl Play!

DOCTOR DOOM. There's room for everyone in the theater.

FREAK. Even me?

CHORUS. Yes!

DOCTOR DOOM. Even you.

FREAK. Wow! I've secretly always wanted to be in the theater.

DOCTOR DOOM. I have a secret too. I am—

DOREEN. Not Doctor Doom.

DOCTOR DOOM. What? How did you know?

DOREEN. You are a Doombot.

TIPPY-TOE. *(to audience)* This is what they call a "cookie" for the serious Marvel Comics fans...

DOREEN. You are a clone of Doctor Doom...

DOCTOR DOOM. Yes...

DOREEN. *And* so much more.

DOCTOR DOOM. How did you know?

DOREEN. Doctor Doom is not self-aware. But you are.

DOCTOR DOOM. I guess I am...

DOREEN. Even a clone has something singular and special that must shine through! Kind of like a nut...

CHORUS. Yes, *and—*

SMARTNOGGIN. But *no!* My bad work is not done! So my new job will be Mean Non-Constructive Theater Critic... and I will destroy this play!

CHORUS. A Squirrel Girl Play!

SMARTNOGGIN. Wait for my review, Squirrel Girl! HA-HA-HA...

(**SMARTNOGGIN** *runs off.*)

DOCTOR DOOM. What should we do about Mean Teacher?

TIPPY-TOE. What should anyone do when someone tries to squash your dreams and individuality?

DOREEN. Do the thing that scares you most!

NANCY. Hug a rodent!

(**NANCY** *gingerly hugs* **TIPPY-TOE.**)

CHORUS. Hug it out!

DOREEN. Yay!

TOMÁS. Doreen... will you... go out with me?

DOREEN. *(big smile)* Yes!

DOCTOR DOOM. *And...*

DOREEN. *(deep breath)* Dance!

EPILOGUE
Theater

(**CHORUS** *leads some music.* **ALL** *dance.*
SMARTNOGGIN *enters writing a terrible
review.*)

CHORUS. *(sung)*
SQUIRREL GIRL, SUPER HERO
SHE'S THE STRONGEST ONE IN THE WORLD
SHE'S UP-FRONT! SHE'S POSITIVE!
FIGURING OUT THE BEST WAY TO LIVE
SQUIRREL GIRL, WATCH OUT!
HERE COMES SQUIRREL GIRL!

DOREEN. In a play!

TIPPY-TOE. The End!

ALL. Nuts Kick Butts!

End of Play

GLOSSARY

Doombot (34): Robots modeled after their creator, Doctor Doom.

Et tu, Brute? (11): "And you, Brutus?" A famous line in Latin from the title character of Shakespeare's *Julius Caesar* as he is murdered by his best friend.

Greek chorus (2, 37, 49): In ancient Greek theater, the chorus was a key part of both tragedy and comedy. It represented the voice of the people and commented on the action of the play, often through song.

"Yes, and..." (5, 22, 27, 28, 30, 33, 34): A core guideline of theatrical improvisation that encourages participants to add to what has come before rather than negate it.

PRODUCTION NOTES

The following pages offer staging, design, and performance suggestions to inform your production of *Squirrel Girl Goes to College*. For more tips and guidance on how to approach the Marvel Spotlight plays in production, visit MarvelSpotlightPlays.com.

Squirrel Girl Goes to College is an homage to theater and employs a wide range of theatrical and meta-theatrical elements and devices, including a Greek chorus, breaking the fourth wall, narration, character descriptions, scene headings, and flashbacks.

Comedy

This play celebrates comedy and practices its core elements: pacing, style, physicality, and... timing. Success in this genre walks a tightrope between precision and flexibility so it can deliver uniquely for each audience, which through audible response plays an essential role in the rhythm of performance. What may look simple on the page will develop many layers in rehearsal, so be brave, dive deep, play around, and make big choices to heighten and deliver both the drama and the comedy in your unique production.

Tippy-Toe and Squirrel Chorus

Tippy-Toe and the Squirrel Chorus play roles both in and outside the drama. Through narration, they frame and comment on the action, but they also help keep the momentum and drive the play forward. Experiment with staging and rhythm in rehearsal to generate maximum fun!

Scenes, Flashbacks, and Monologues

Because the Squirrels announce scenes, flashbacks, and monologues – and can ignite audience imagination with only their words – very little is required of your set. You may find a couple of large rolling frames (reminiscent of

comics panels) useful for stepping in and outside of the action. Keep furniture to a minimum so scene transitions can be quick, if not instantaneous.

Music

Squirrel Chorus-generated rhythm and music is an important part of the play that should be devised uniquely by your ensemble. Leave plenty of time to rehearse what you generate so it can be executed precisely in performance.

Computer Science

The "computer science" represented in the play is sketchy at best. *Do not* try at home to clone a tree or steal people's abilities with wired helmets!

Final Scene

Classic comedies end in a long final scene in which all the characters end up on stage and all of the plot complications are resolved. *Squirrel Girl Goes to College* is no exception. The key to a successful ending is *pace*, so keep things moving!

BEYOND THE STAGE

Facilitating a productive rehearsal process isn't just about having clear rehearsal plans, it's also about meaningful engagement and ensuring the well-being of your cast. It's important your cast feels physically, emotionally, and artistically safe throughout the rehearsal process. The following pages include resources to help:

- In-Rehearsal Discussion Starters
- Rehearsal Exercises
- Post-Show Talkbacks

For best practices on stage combat and to ensure the physical safety of your performers, ideas on how to make the Marvel Universe theatrical, and additional exercises to connect to the world of comics, go to MarvelSpotlightPlays.com.

In-Rehearsal Discussion Starters

Throughout the rehearsal process, help your cast make deeper connections to the play and their characters using the following prompts:

- How are Doreen's strengths different from those of Squirrel Girl?
- What is challenging about making friends in a completely new context like college? What external and internal forces impact what the characters share with one another? What are the factors that influence what personal details you share with your friends?
- Heroism often has a cost. What sacrifices does our hero make? What sacrifices would you be willing to make in exchange for super powers?

The director's job is not only to helm the vision of the show, but also to assist actors in developing a bond as an ensemble, introduce them to the world of the play, and guide them to join the storytelling process.

Below are a wide variety of exercises that will help with that. For even more rehearsal exercises, visit MarvelSpotlightPlays.com.

OWNING YOUR IDENTITY (AND YOUR MOVES)

Use this to: *help your ensemble members get to know one another and understand themes from* Squirrel Girl Goes to College.

Doreen Green hides her super hero identity to protect her new friends from a super villain who threatened to harm people close to her. Ask your actors to choose one thing about themselves that they are proud of. Next, prompt them to think of an original dance move that represents this aspect of themselves. Allow them a moment to practice owning their dance move and then turn on some music for a dance party! One at a time, invite each actor to share their move in the center of the circle, with the rest of the cast supporting them by also trying out the dance move. Repeat this activity as a warm-up throughout your rehearsals, encouraging your cast to explore new aspects of themselves that they are proud of.

Apply to rehearsal: by using your cast's original dance moves when choreographing Doreen and Modoc's dance-off or the play's final dance party.

FEELING SQUIRREL-Y

Use this to: *explore how to physicalize the qualities of squirrels as both animal and human characters.*

Invite your actors to move freely about the space, encouraging them to walk as they typically would. After the group has settled, ask them to take note of how they move, how the floor feels beneath their feet, how their bodies move through space, what part or area of their bodies seems to lead them, etc. Share with your actors that this is them moving at 100% human. Then, share with your cast that they have been endowed with squirrel-like powers, and that they should move as if they are 75% human and 25% squirrel. Allow actors time to explore and move before prompting them to move as if they are 50% human and 50% squirrel. Next, prompt your actors to move as if they are 25% human and 75% squirrel. Finally, end the activity by asking each actor to individually transform into a frozen image that is 100% squirrel.

Apply to rehearsal: by leading the actors playing Doreen Green and the Squirrel Chorus through this activity to establish a movement vocabulary. Side coach your actors to consider how their squirrel-like movements might shift depending on the scene and circumstance.

CONSIDERING THE CHORUS

Use this to: *help your actors examine the role of a Greek chorus and how they work together to narrate the action of a play.*

Share with your cast that *Squirrel Girl Goes to College* uses the theatrical device of a Greek chorus to help tell the story. Review the following goals of a Greek chorus:

- The chorus narrates the story, often speaking and moving in unison in an exaggerated fashion.
- They comment on themes, the unsaid secrets, thoughts, and fears of the main characters, and provide other characters with information.

Divide your cast into groups of five actors and give each group a mundane every day activity (e.g., walking to class, choosing an outfit, studying for a test, etc.). Prompt the groups to write five to six sentences narrating that activity in the style of a Greek chorus. After they have written their narration, invite the chorus to rehearse their performance, with one member of the group stepping out to pantomime the activity. As time allows, invite the groups to share their work.

Apply to rehearsal: by identifying which sections use narration and practicing how the Squirrel Chorus can ideally interact with other characters' blocking to tell the story on stage.

Post-Show Talkbacks

Post-Show Talkbacks encourage audiences to forge deeper connections with your production. The following prompts can help start the conversation:

- What human strengths do the characters possess? How are they related to those of a super hero?
- What does this play teach us about the origin of a villain? How does this villain's early experiences influence their trajectory?

SQUIRREL GIRL ORIGIN SKETCH

The following sketch introduces Doreen Green as Squirrel Girl as a way to promote *Squirrel Girl Goes to College*. It can be performed anywhere that attracts an audience (the cafeteria, for example) or filmed and posted on the school or theater's website. It can even be played or performed pre-show in order to familiarize your audience with our hero. Additionally, consider publishing The Origin of Squirrel Girl (p. V) in your program.

(**TIPPY-TOE** *enters with* **SQUIRREL CHORUS.**)

TIPPY-TOE. Attention! I am Tippy-Toe and I have a very important introduction.

CHORUS. Introduction!

TIPPY-TOE. Please meet... the incredible Doreen Green.

> (**DOREEN** *enters, surprised by her appearance.*)

DOREEN. What is happening?! I look like a... squirrel!

CHORUS. And we are a Squirrel Chorus!

TIPPY-TOE. Doreen Green, there's no easy way to break this to you... but at every point in a young girl's life, she realizes that she has powers... powers that she can hide... or powers that she can harness and unleash to the world in all their fierce magic.

DOREEN. Okay...

TIPPY-TOE. And today is the day you realize that you, Doreen Green, have all the powers of a *squirrel*... but in a girl!

CHORUS. Ooohhh!

DOREEN. What? Are you saying that out of all the animals in the world – spider, ant, wasp, black widow, kangaroo, rhino, tarantula – that I get *(very excited) squirrel* super powers?

TIPPY-TOE. Yes! Sorry! Not sorry. But yes.

CHORUS. Ooohhh!

TIPPY-TOE. I know squirrels aren't as elite and majestic as other animals, but...

CHORUS. But...?

DOREEN. Do you know how self-conscious I would feel if I had to be like Tiger Girl and wear a slinky, tight cat suit? Squirrels are low-key and great! Give me a comfortable pair of pants and some kick-ass boots and let me change the world.

TIPPY-TOE. I can't tell you how much the world needs a squirrel super hero like you.

DOREEN. Tell me!

CHORUS. Tell us!

TIPPY-TOE. What if I told you that you, Doreen Green, have the potential of being the most powerful super hero in the Marvel Universe?

CHORUS. Ooohhh!

TIPPY-TOE. What if I told you that your warm wit, smart vibes, and positive personality will overwhelm even the worst super villain?

CHORUS. Ooohhh!

TIPPY-TOE. The super villain world is aflutter with fear. Your joy, power, and sense of adventure are a big threat to any doom-and-gloom, wanna-take-over-the-universe types.

DOREEN. People underestimate the power of girls at their peril.

CHORUS. And squirrels!

DOREEN. Right! What other animal is as cute, agile, and strong, and has enough foresight to save acorns? Squirrels think of the future.

TIPPY-TOE. The Future Is Squirrel.

CHORUS. Squirrel Girl!

TIPPY-TOE. This is going so much better than I imagined.

DOREEN. Being Squirrel Girl is going to make high school so much more interesting. And it's a great extra-curricular for my college application!

TIPPY-TOE. Hey! *Squirrel Girl Goes to College* is the play we are putting on!

DOREEN. How exciting! When? Where? How?

TIPPY-TOE. *(insert show details, or if performed pre-show:)* Now! Here! Like this!

CHORUS. Starring you!

(**DOREEN** *poses as* **SQUIRREL GIRL.**)

DOREEN. A Squirrel Girl Play!

CHORUS. You'd be nuts to miss it!

End of Sketch